P9-DOG-076

CRUSHER
THE CREEPING TERROR

With special thanks to Brandon Robshaw

www.seaquestbooks.co.uk

ORCHARD BOOKS

First published in Great Britain in 2013 by Orchard Books
This edition published in 2016 by The Watts Publishing Group

3 5 7 9 10 8 6 4

Text © 2013 Beast Quest Limited.
Cover and inside illustrations by Artful Doodlers with special thanks to Bob and Justin
© Orchard Books 2013

Illustrations copyright Artful Doodlers with special thanks to Bob and Justin, 2013

Series created by Beast Quest Limited, London

The moral rights of the author and illustrator have been asserted.

A CIP catalogue record for this book is available from the British Library.

ISBN 978 1 40832 413 4

Printed in Great Britain by Clays Ltd, St Ives plc

MIX
Paper from
responsible sources
FSC® C104740

The paper and board used in this book are made from wood from responsible sources

Orchard Books
An imprint of Hachette Children's Group
Part of The Watts Publishing Group Limited
Carmelite House, 50 Victoria Embankment, London EC4Y 0DZ

An Hachette UK Company
www.hachette.co.uk
www.hachettechildrens.co.uk

CRUSHER
THE CREEPING TERROR

BY ADAM BLADE

ORCHARD

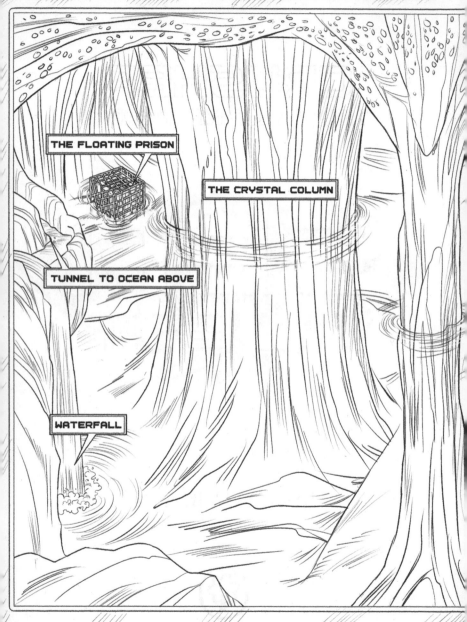

TEN YEARS EARLIER . . .

SPECTRON, 3,548 FATHOMS DEEP,
THE CAVERN OF GHOSTS

I've done it! At last I perfected my new invention. When the Professor strikes, I believe it could foil his evil plan…

Now I must find him. Someone has to stop him, and nobody knows him as well as I do. It will be hard to leave the Sea Ghosts unprotected. They are so kind and innocent, and have shared everything with me, all of their carefully collected treasures of the sea. I fear that they have even come to think of me as their guardian.

But I must leave if their world is to be saved. I can only hope that my new device will be enough to stop the Professor.

If it isn't, the Cavern of Ghosts — and everything that lies above — is doomed…

>LOG ENTRY ENDS

CHAPTER ONE
THE BLACK BOX

"You really knew my mother?" Max said.

"Aye," Roger said. "I knew her."

Max sat in his aquabuggy, ready to leave Spectron, the city of the Sea Ghosts, with his pet dogbot Rivet, his Merryn friend Lia and her swordfish, Spike. Together they had just defeated Stinger – the deadly jellyfish Robobeast created by Max's evil uncle, the Professor, to terrorise Spectron. The giant, broken form of Stinger drifted in the current above the undersea city, no longer glowing with light. Its dangling tentacles hung above the wrecked ships that were the Sea Ghosts' homes. But Max wasn't looking at the jellyfish any more, for he was too shocked and surprised. He had just been told that his missing mother had been seen only a year ago.

Max stared at Roger, the man with the eye patch and ponytail they'd met on their travels, who claimed he wasn't a pirate even though he looked and spoke exactly like one. Roger had just offered to take Max and his friends to the place where he'd met Max's mother. Max couldn't wait to get going, but Roger was busy checking his rocketboots were still in working order.

"So – how did you meet her?" Max asked.

"We travelled together for a while," Roger said. "I met her in the Crystal Forest, a day's journey to the east, on the other side of the mountains."

Max's heart beat faster. He looked down at the conch shell he held in his hands. It had been modified with some kind of electronics – there were wires and buttons and circuits inside, but he had no idea what they did. It had been made and left here by his mother, the Sea Ghosts had told him. Max had begun this quest to defeat the Professor, and had never expected to find out so much about his long-lost mum. It seemed as if every clue pointed back to her.

"Well, come on then," Max said to Roger. "I'm ready when you are!"

He heard Lia tut to herself. She pulled at his arm, and he swam with her a little distance away. They stopped behind a wrecked submarine, just out of Roger's hearing.

"Are you sure it's a good idea to go with

Roger?" Lia asked. "I mean, he's a pirate."

"We don't know that," Max said.

"We need to find the Professor, Max. He's out to destroy this world. And don't forget, if he makes the cavern roof collapse, Sumara will be destroyed too. He's sure to have more Robobeasts ready to attack – we have to stop him!"

"I know," Max said regretfully. He was desperate to learn more about his mother. But he knew Lia was right. He looked up at the giant form of Stinger, floating above them. Inside its pink, transparent body, among the circuits of its computer, he saw a square black object he hadn't noticed before. He pointed. "Hey – what do you think that is?"

"I have no idea," Lia said. "Some sort of technology, I suppose." Like all the Merryn, Lia didn't understand technology, and she

didn't like it either.

"I think it's a black box," Max said. "It's for recording where the jellyfish has been, like the DiveLog from my mum's submarine."

Lia shrugged. "So?"

"If we can pull it out, it should have a record of where Stinger's come from – and that'll tell us where the Professor is!"

Lia screwed up her face in disgust. "Pull it out? That means burrowing through that horrible goo." When they had battled Stinger, both Max and Lia had become all too familiar with the goo that made up the jellyfish's body. It had a nasty habit of lodging in their gills, making it impossible to breathe.

"Not fun," Max agreed. "But how else can we track the Professor?"

"Well...all right, then," Lia said at last. "As long as you're the one who goes in to get it!"

"I had a feeling you might say that," Max said.

He put the electronic conch away in the storage compartment of his aquabuggy.

"Ready now," Roger announced.

"Just a minute," Max told him. He swam up to the massive form of Stinger, together with Lia, Spike and Rivet. The black box was dimly visible behind a thick wall of pink jelly. Stinger's tentacles waved gently in the current.

"It is dead, isn't it?" Lia said.

"It was never really alive," Max said. "But I think it's pretty much done for."

Lia tapped Spike on the back. "Go on, Spike – cut out a way to that black box."

The swordfish darted at Stinger's body, and its sharp bill sliced a long slit in the pink goo.

"In you go, Max!" Lia said.

Max gulped. He wasn't going to enjoy this. He took a deep breath, shut his mouth firmly and pushed his way into the gooey hole Spike had created.

The jelly was thick, warm and sticky, clinging to his arms and legs. It was hard to tell whether he was making progress. The black box hardly seemed to get any nearer. Soon Max couldn't breathe. The goo had coated his gills so thickly that no water could come in.

I must grab that box and get out, Max thought. *I need to breathe...*

Using all his strength, he dragged himself nearer to the box. His fingers grazed it, and then, finally, he was able to clutch it in both hands.

He began to move backwards. He couldn't wait for the moment when he would breathe in cool water through his gills again.

Suddenly, Max felt the jelly walls around him twitch, pressing in on him and gripping him tight. What was happening?

Stinger's deactivated, he thought, *but I must've triggered some sort of robotic reflex. It won't let me go – but if I don't get out fast, I'll suffocate!*

He thrashed his arms and legs. But he wasn't going anywhere. The urge to breathe

was overwhelming – but there was nothing
he could do...

Suddenly, he felt a tug on the back of
his suit. Faintly, he could hear propellers
whirling. He was being pulled backwards. If

he could just hold on a little longer...

The world seemed to change from pink to green as Rivet dragged him clear of Stinger and into the open water. Max spluttered, wiping the goo from his gills, then gulped in water. He handed the black box to Lia.

"Thanks, Riv!" he gasped.

"No problem, Max," the dogbot barked.

"Are you okay? How do we use this?" Lia asked. She touched a button on the black box and its screen lit up, startling her.

"I'll be fine. Let's see," said Max, still getting his breath back. The screen showed a map with Spectron marked on it, and a dotted line heading east over the mountains and through the Crystal Forest. "Look – Stinger came the same way Roger's going to take us. We can kill two birds with one stone!"

"What are 'birds'?" Lia asked.

"It's an Aquoran expression. I mean, we

can go after the Professor, and at the same time go with Roger to look for my mum."

Lia sighed. "Very well," she said. "But I'm going to keep an eye on that pirate."

"I heard that!" Roger said, swimming up to them, powered by his rocketboots. "How many times do I have to tell you, shipmates, I ain't a pirate!"

Max led the way back to the ocean floor, and put the black box away in the aquabuggy. "Let's get going!" he said. He revved up the engine. "Jump on, Rivet!"

"Wait!" called a voice. It was Ko, the Sea Ghost boy they had befriended. He came swimming up to the adventurers, at the head of a large group of Sea Ghosts. "You not leave without thanks. You save Mother's life – and you save our city from monster."

"It's clear that you are your mother's son," said an old Sea Ghost.

"Please take gifts," Ko said. All of the Sea Ghosts were holding out small treasures scavenged from shipwrecks: plastic toys, buttons and small coins, fizzy drink cans, a necklace of dead batteries, jewellery fashioned from safety pins and paperclips.

"What a load of junk!" Roger muttered.

Max glared at him. "It's not junk!" he hissed. The strange items clearly meant a lot to the Sea Ghosts. Max was touched. "Thank you," he said, as he took the objects. "We'll see you again, Ko, I promise! Very soon."

He took one last look at the crowd of pale green, semi-transparent Sea Ghosts, floating above their shipwreck homes, and waved. Then he turned on the aquabuggy's engine. Below, half buried under the sand, he caught a glimpse of the strange, smooth ocean floor. It was skin, he was almost sure of it – which meant Spectron was built on top of some creature. Max had heard something from below which sounded like a colossal heart beating. If there *was* a creature, it had to be huge...

"Come on!" Lia said. "Let's get moving!"

Roger was already zooming ahead to the east, powered by his rocketboots. Max pressed down on the accelerator pedal and the aquabuggy roared into life, with Lia and Spike swimming by his side and Rivet perched on the back seat.

His heart pounded. A new adventure was beginning. He had a feeling they would face the Professor again soon. And this time, Max was determined to find out what had happened to his mother.

CHAPTER TWO

GRUNDLE MUSIC

"We should stop to rest," Lia said as they travelled over the mountains. "And eat."

She's right, Max thought. They would need to keep their strength up. They had been going for hours. Below them, a sharp ridge of jagged black peaks sloped away into a dark valley.

"Let's stop down there," Max said. "It'll be sheltered from the ocean currents."

"All right then," Roger replied. "But let's make it snappy. You're not the only ones wanting to find the Professor, you know. I've got a score or two to settle with him."

Lia frowned at him. "We're not going to rush," she said. She hated being told what to do, Max knew. In Sumara she was a princess, and not used to taking orders.

They landed on the lower slopes of the valley, and Lia got out the bag of seaweed cakes they had brought.

The sight of the cakes made Max's mouth water. When he'd first tasted the Merryn's favourite food, soon after arriving in Sumara, he'd thought they were horrible. But now he quite enjoyed them. He grabbed one and took a big bite. A horrible, mildewed taste filled his mouth. He spat it out. "Ugh!" he said. "They've gone bad!"

"Rubbish!" Lia said. "There's nothing wrong with these lovely cakes. You just don't appreciate them because you're a Breather."

She took a bite of one, and then she too spat it out in disgust.

"What's the matter?" Max said. "Don't you appreciate the lovely cakes?"

Lia inspected the cake. "All right," she said. "Maybe they are past their best..."

Max looked at what was left of his cake. It was covered in grey patches. "They've gone mouldy!" Now he was getting worried. All of the cakes looked inedible, but they would have to eat something. Where would they get more food?

Rivet cocked his head, as if locating a sound.

"What is it, Riv?" Max asked.

"Noise, Max!"

Max listened hard. From far away, he heard a haunting music. It sounded as if it was being played by twangy stringed instruments, and it was slow and sad, but incredibly beautiful. Max felt a kind of warm, familiar feeling, as if he recognised the melody from some distant memory. "Anyone else hear that?"

Roger tilted his head to listen, then groaned. "Oh no! It's the Grundle!"

"The what?" Max and Lia said together.

"They're a nomadic species," Roger said. "They travel the ocean, setting up camp and playing their weird music. It attracts travellers – no idea why. I've never seen the point of it myself – give me a good old sea shanty any day! But most people can't get enough of it. The only thing is, once they catch you listening, you have to pay a toll."

"What sort of toll?" Max asked.

"Doesn't matter, as long as it's useful to them," Roger said. "Tools, food, jewellery, weapons, whatever. But you have to give them something, or they'll make you sorry. People think they're a soft touch, with their plinky-plonky music, but they have a nasty side, believe me."

The music was slowly growing louder. Max thought it was a beautiful sound. It made him feel happy, sleepy and comfortable. "Why don't we stop here for a bit?" he said. "We'll go and see the Grundle and listen to the music properly."

"We might be able to get some food from them," Lia said.

"And the toll?" Roger said.

"There must be something we can give them," Max said. "We'll think about that later." He was desperate to hear more of the music.

"All right," Roger said. "But we'd better be ready to get out of here fast, if they turn nasty."

"Don't worry, they won't," Max said, as he swam towards the music. He couldn't believe that people who made such beautiful sounds could ever be dangerous.

The Grundle had set up camp in a sandy area surrounded on three sides by rocks. They looked rather like rocks themselves – large, brownish-grey creatures with rough skin, craggy features and big sad eyes. They sat around a glowing piece of red coral which gave off heat, playing strange instruments:

drums made from shells, and stringed instruments with strands of seaweed drawn tight over the skulls of marine animals. Other travellers had stopped to listen to the music too. Max saw several Sea Ghosts, and a group of creatures he hadn't seen before: pale, plump little gnomes with fins and long squirmy noses, like elephants' trunks. The trunks swayed dreamily in time to the music.

The Grundle bowed gravely when they saw Max and his friends, then carried on playing. Max, Roger and Rivet settled down on the sand to listen. Even Rivet seemed to enjoy the music, wagging his tail to the rhythm.

"I'm going to go and see if I can get some food," Lia said. She and Spike swam to the other side of the camp where there were several stalls.

Max settled in and gave himself up to the music. It was twangy, thumpy, haunting and

sad, yet comforting. Listening to it, he felt as if he understood the mystery of life.

"You look like you're away with the mermaids!" Roger said. "You're under the Grundle spell – you want to snap out of it, Max my lad."

"I'm just enjoying the music," Max said with a smile.

Soon Lia and Spike returned with a bag of food, though Max hadn't been aware of any

time passing. "They've got all sorts of stuff there," Lia said. "Fish, octopus, sea snails, everything." She made a disgusted face. "But we don't like eating animals, do we, Spike? So we got more seaweed cakes."

"They cater to travellers," Roger said. "But it'll come out of the toll."

"Shh!" Max said. "I'm trying to listen."

All too soon, it seemed, the music ended. Two of the Grundle stood up – they really were big, Max realised – and made their way around the audience, holding out a large empty shell. The Sea Ghosts and the long-nosed gnomes dropped coins and trinkets into the shell. Max wondered what to give. He'd hand over anything, as long as he could hear more of that lovely music.

An idea came to him. As the Grundle approached, Max reached into the aquabuggy's storage compartment and drew out a handful of the gifts the Sea Ghosts had given him.

Lia frowned. "Are you sure you want to give those away, Max?" she said. "They were presents."

"Of course I'm sure," Max said. What were a few trinkets, compared to that wonderful music?

The Grundle looked at the gifts Max was holding out, and shook their heads sadly.

They jiggled the shell up and down.

"What's wrong?" Max asked.

"They don't think much of the Sea Ghosts' junk," Roger said. "And I don't blame them."

What else can we offer? Max thought. And then he remembered the stinger they had taken from the robo-jellyfish. He pulled it out of the aquabuggy and showed it to Lia. It was a long piece of synthetic tissue – it felt soft but muscular, like a snake, but slightly sticky. The electric sting at the end glowed bright pink. "What do you think?" he said. "We've already got the hyperblade from Shredder – do we really need this?"

"Belay there!" Roger said sharply. "You've got the jellyfish's stinger? That's a powerful weapon, you can't give them that!"

But it was too late. The Grundle had picked up the stinger and were examining it. They nodded at each other. It was too big to go

into the collecting shell, so one of them put it over his shoulder.

"Hooray! Now they'll play for us again!" Max said.

"No, we'd better go now," Lia said, gently prodding Max's shoulder. "We've got our provisions."

She doesn't seem to appreciate the music,

Max thought. "Can't we stay and listen some more?" he said.

"No, let's get out of here before you give the aquabuggy away!" Roger said. "Hold on, me hearties, I just want to get something from the food stall – you go, I'll catch you up."

Reluctantly, Max stood and left the circle. He settled into the aquabuggy and revved the engine, and they left the camp, heading east. As they got further away from the Grundle encampment, Max missed the music less and less. He could feel his head clearing. What had he given as a toll, again? He was finding it hard to remember.

Roger caught them up just at the edge of the mountain range, carrying a waterproof backpack.

"What did you get from the food stall?" Lia asked him.

"Oh, er – they didn't have anything I wanted," Roger said quickly, as he stowed the bag in the aquabuggy.

Max was just about to ask what was in the bag when Rivet cocked his head again. "Music, Max!"

Max listened. The beautiful music had started up again. He slowed the aquabuggy down, wanting to hear more...

"No, full sail ahead!" Roger said. "We'd better get out of here, fast."

"Why?" Max asked.

"Just do it!"

The music grew louder and louder even though they were moving away. Suddenly a crowd of Grundle shot through the water at alarming speed, still holding their instruments, and surrounded them.

The Grundle stopped playing. Their faces were twisted with anger.

"You bad men!" One of them, a big square creature with a face that looked like it was carved out of grey granite, spoke in a deep, booming voice, in the Merryn language. "You try to cheat the Grundle!"

CHAPTER THREE

THE TOLL

"Now we're for it," Roger groaned. "You should have got out of there quicker, boy. I warned you."

"Why?" Max said. Now that the music had stopped his head had cleared again. "What's the matter?"

The Grundle moved closer, hemming them in like a towering wall of rock. The largest one spoke again. "You stole from us. The Grundle do not like thieves. The Grundle punish thieves."

"There must be a mistake," Roger said quickly. "I expect you just lost the... whatever it is."

"We're not thieves!" Lia said.

"And we are not fools!" the big grey Grundle boomed. His companions moved in closer, cutting off any chance of escape, muttering in low voices. They were huge, and they outnumbered Max and his friends by at least four to one. *If they decided to crush us*, Max thought, *we'd have no chance.*

"The boy gave us an unusual stinging weapon," the grey Grundle said. "That weapon is gone. You give it back to us – or we take something."

Lia glared at Roger. "Did you take the stinger?"

"Me?" said Roger, spreading his arms and opening his one eye wide.

Another Grundle pounced on Max's

electronic conch, which was lying on the passenger seat of the aquabuggy. "We will take this!"

"No!" Max said. He grabbed the conch from the Grundle. He didn't know what the shell could do, but it had been his mother's and he wasn't going to give it up.

The big square Grundle nodded at the one next to it, which was slightly thinner, and brown. The brown Grundle's hand shot out and gripped Max by the neck. He felt its huge, stony fingers pressing against his gills, sealing them. He couldn't breathe.

Rivet growled at the Grundle. It took no notice.

"You give us the conch!" boomed the grey Grundle.

"I – can't!" Max gasped. "Take something else, but—"

The grip on his throat tightened. Max

gasped and choked.

Rivet shot forward and chomped down
on the Grundle's leg. But his iron jaws
didn't even scratch the creature's rock-like
hide. The Grundle seized Rivet with its
free hand and pushed him away. Lia swam

forward, but another Grundle grabbed hold of her, so she couldn't move.

"Avast there!" Roger said. "Leave the boy."

He took out a knife from his belt and offered it to the creature, hilt-first. "Here, take this. It's solid vernium."

The big grey Grundle looked at it. "Not enough."

Roger sighed. He bent down and took off his boot. Inside was a bag of gold coins. They clinked as he handed it over. "All right?"

The Grundle inspected the coins. At last he nodded. The grip on Max's neck loosened. He spluttered and breathed deeply.

"Don't come near our camp again," boomed the grey Grundle. "You are not welcome any more."

Moving as one, they swam away as

abruptly as they had arrived. Max watched their big, bulky bodies fade away in the green gloom, thankful to see the back of them. He touched his bruised neck gingerly.

"You owe me a knife and twelve gold credits, boy," Roger said.

Lia put her hands on her hips. "You took that stinger, didn't you? It's inside that backpack."

Roger nodded. "Too right I did. It's a powerful weapon – it would have been crazy to give it away, especially when you don't know what else the Professor has in store." He flipped open the storage compartment of the aquabuggy and took the stinger out of the bag. "Here it is. Aren't you glad we've still got it? You must have been under the spell of the Grundle music, or you'd never have given away advanced technology like this."

Max thought about it. Maybe Roger was right. But he still felt angry. "You should have offered the knife and the coins first off," he said to Roger. "Stealing the stinger back was dishonest! And because of you I nearly lost the conch shell that my mum—" He stopped, feeling too upset to talk. The conch shell was the only memento of his mother he had, and he didn't even know what it did.

He felt Lia's hand upon his shoulder. "Don't worry, you still have the conch."

Roger was staring at him oddly. "You're very different from your mother, aren't you?"

"What do you mean?" Max demanded. "How well did you know her?"

"Very well," Roger said. "We got along fine. We were in the same line of business, you might say."

"You mean she was a pirate?" Lia asked.

Max didn't like that idea. Of course his mother wasn't a pirate. He looked anxiously at Roger, waiting for his answer.

"In fact, no," Roger said, "because I am not a pirate, as I keep telling you. Let's just say that Max's mother had a taste for danger. Like me."

A taste for danger, Max thought. *Yes, she*

must have had that, or she wouldn't have gone exploring under the sea all those years ago.

Max carefully strapped the conch back on to his aquabuggy and they set off again. As they headed east towards the Crystal Forest, he kept thinking about Roger's words. *A taste for danger.* He'd only been two years old when his mother left, so he didn't remember her well. But Roger was suggesting she was reckless, someone who sought out risks. And who was in the same line of business as Roger, whatever that meant. Surely she wasn't a pirate! But could his mother have been so different from his careful, cautious father? The thought was disturbing, but also oddly exciting. *Maybe that's where I get my own taste for adventure from*, Max thought.

Perhaps he'd find out more on this quest. Maybe Roger would lead him to the truth.

The aquabuggy zoomed through the ocean. Max could see schools of pale, ghostly-looking fish up ahead. And in the far distance, glinting silver in the dim green water, was a group of tall, parallel columns, reaching up high.

The Crystal Forest.

CHAPTER FOUR

THE CRYSTAL FOREST

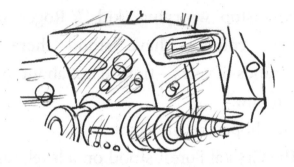

As they got closer, Max saw that the crystal columns went right up to the surface of the water, and beyond.

"They go up to the roof of the cavern?" he asked Roger.

"That's right, boy. All the way up."

Max glanced at Lia. "Like the giant one we saw near the Professor's floating prison," he said. "They must be holding up the roof of the whole Cavern of Ghosts."

Lia nodded. "And if anything happened to them, that great mass of rock would come down. Hydrophantia would be destroyed. And so would Sumara."

"Oh, stop worrying, kids!" Roger said. "Those columns have stood there for thousands of years – they're not about to fall down now."

Max hoped he was right.

The Crystal Forest stood on a level, sandy floor. Behind the forest, the ocean floor dropped away abruptly, like the edge of a shelf. Max could not see beyond it – there was no slope downwards, just a sheer drop.

Dotted around the Forest there were large, smooth, rounded black rocks. It was a strange and eerie landscape.

"So this is where you met my mother?" Max asked.

"Right here," Roger said.

"What was she doing here?"

Roger was about to reply when Lia interrupted them.

"Look!" she cried. "Those black things—"

Max's gaze followed the direction of her pointing finger. Now they were closer, he could see scores of little black figures swarming around the base of the crystal columns – and he heard a buzzing sound. Were the figures harming the columns? He gunned the engine of the aquabuggy and accelerated.

The black figures were small, squat robots, each no bigger than an infant. They had boxy bodies and bright white electric eyes. Attachments on their stumpy arms secured electric drills which buzzed like a swarm of angry bees. Sure enough, they were attacking the crystal columns. The water was filled with tiny, glittering shards of the crystal, and

some of the robots were collecting it and
storing it in carts.

As Max watched, the robot right in front of
him dug deep with its drill, and a crack ran
right up the column. More pieces of crystal
broke free and floated in the water. Then
Max saw that there was a whole network of

these little cracks, running right up towards the top of the column.

"The cracks are going higher and higher!" Lia cried. "The column's going to break up!"

Roger laughed. "Get your priorities right. This our chance to get rich, don't you see that? I wish your mother was here, Max! She'd have hated to miss this!"

"What do you mean?" Max demanded.

"That crystal's valuable, Max lad," said Roger. "By weight, it's worth more than diamonds. It's hard to break it away from the columns without special tools. But since someone's going to all the trouble of mining it for us, we can fill our pockets!"

Roger's jet-powered diving boots propelled him forward. He began to gather up every shard of crystal he could find, and shove them into the pockets of his deepsuit.

Max and Lia looked at each other. "This

is the Professor's work," Max said. "He can use the crystal to pay for his schemes. And at the same time he's weakening the columns, so he can bring the roof down and destroy Hydrophantia and Sumara!"

"He's trying to kill two stones with one bird," Lia said.

"Well, almost," Max said. "But the important thing is, we're going to stop him!"

CHAPTER FIVE

CRUSHER AWAKES

Max saw that the column nearest them was in the worst state of all. Great chunks had been hacked out, and what was left was covered in a network of cracks. Several of the robots were working on it, repeatedly attacking the crystal with their drills. Each time they struck, the column shook, sending shock waves all around. And if one column went, the remaining ones would be under even more stress.

"That one's going to go, and soon," he said to Lia, "unless we do something – fast. I'll try to stop the robots. Can you and Spike keep the column propped up?"

"We'll stop it falling if it kills us!" Lia said. "I won't let the Professor destroy my city!" She and Spike swam straight up to where the column reached the surface of the water.

"Roger!" Max called. "Can you help?"

Roger looked round briefly. "I'm kind of busy here." He swam off and caught an especially large piece of crystal that had just been broken off.

"Great," Max said. "Thanks for the help." He turned to Rivet instead. "Come on, boy," he said.

Max grabbed the super-sized hyperblade that he'd got from the leg of Shredder the Spider Droid. Then he and the dogbot went straight for the two nearest mining robots.

Max swung the hyperblade at one robot and struck it just where the head and body joined. There was a clang as the robot's head came clean off and floated down to the ocean floor. But its mechanical arm went on operating the drill.

Max chopped with the blade again, cutting off the robot's arm.

Rivet grabbed the other robot's arm in his metal jaws and pulled it away from the column. He shook until the robot let the drill fall.

The robots didn't fight back. *They're just dumb machines, programmed to drill and nothing else*, Max realised. That was strange. It wasn't like the Professor to leave his mining operation undefended.

"Help!" Lia called. "We can't hold it much longer!"

Max looked up and saw that Lia and

Spike were braced against the column, Lia with her back to it and Spike pushing with his bill. Spike's tail flapped with the effort of trying to hold such a huge object upright. And it wasn't working. The column was tilting sharply. Larger and larger pieces were falling off it.

"Come on, Riv!" Max swam upwards to help.

They reached Lia and Spike. Max pushed against the crystal with both hands. He felt the massive weight push back, and he knew it was too late.

There was a mighty cracking sound.

"Shiver me timbers!" Roger cried. Out of the corner of his eye, Max saw him zoom away from the column.

The whole thing was breaking up and collapsing.

"We can't save it now!" Max shouted to

the others. "Get clear!"

They pushed away and swam into clearer waters.

The next moment there was an enormous *whooomph!* The top part of the column that had reached up to the roof was no longer supported. It crashed down into the sea and plunged towards the ocean bed, spinning the currents into an underwater tornado.

Max was whirled away by the shock wave. He couldn't see. He was blinded by silt, buffeted by fragments of rock, tipped upside down.

His hyperblade was ripped from his hand and went spinning away.

The currents dragged him back down to the ocean floor.

Max hit solid ground with a thump, found his feet and stood up, trying to rub the silt from his eyes and choking as currents rushed past him.

At last the scene cleared a little. He still couldn't see much. The water was clouded with sand and rock. Big chunks of crystal were tumbling to the ocean floor. Max shielded his eyes and saw one directly above him, coming down fast.

At the last second he darted away. The crystal landed where he'd just been standing, making a great dent in the sand and throwing up more clouds of debris.

He couldn't see Lia, or Spike, or Roger.

There was a snuffling sound and Rivet came paddling up to him, propellers whirling. Max patted his head. "Am I glad to see you, boy!" He was about to call out for the others when he noticed something.

The smooth black rocks he'd seen earlier were moving. *Must be quite a current*, Max thought, *to shift rocks that size.*

But then he saw that there was something purposeful about the way the rocks were moving. They weren't being buffeted about randomly. They were coming together. As if seeking each other.

There were about twenty of them, and they formed a loose semi-circle around Max. *They're targeting me*, he thought, and felt a jolt of dread.

Spiky legs shot out from the underside of each rock. Suddenly they didn't look like rocks any more. They looked more like creatures. Giant crabs, or sea urchins.

They scuttled closer together.

Max saw steel tendrils shoot out from each segment. The tendrils met and interlocked, pulling the segments together with clicks. In a few instants they had formed one long, segmented creature. The underside of each section glowed a bright green.

The Robobeast's front segment reared up. Two eyes opened and emitted a yellow light. The head turned and looked straight at Max, and its jagged mouth opened and shut greedily.

The word CRUSHER was carved into its forehead, just above the eyes.

Max's blood turned to ice.

So the Professor didn't leave his mining

operation undefended after all, he thought. *He put this Robobeast here to guard it. A giant, underwater centipede!*

CHAPTER SIX

TRAPPED

Crusher half surrounded him, like a horseshoe. Max began to back away, but the Robobeast's eyes flared brighter, and it let out a loud buzzing sound. Its legs scrabbled over the ocean floor, carrying it ever closer so that Max couldn't get away.

"Max!"

It was Lia's voice. The silt had settled and the water was clearer now. She was standing behind him, not far away, with Spike, who seemed to be lying on the ground. They were both inside the encircling coil of the centipede's body.

Max swam over to his friend. The centipede tracked him, buzzing like a great robotic wasp. The green glow followed it like a lurid shadow.

"Lia – are you OK?"

Lia was fighting back tears. "Look – look what's happened to Spike!'

A massive piece of crystal had landed on

one of the swordfish's side-fins, pinning him to the seabed. The sand around the fin was soaked red with blood. Spike's other side-fin fluttered feebly and his big round eyes gazed up at Lia. Rivet came and stood near Spike, and gave an electronic whine. "Poor fish," he said.

Max tried to lift the chunk of crystal. Not a chance – it was far too heavy.

Then he had an idea. "Rivet – can you dig around it? If you can make a hollow underneath, Spike could pull his fin clear."

"Yes, Max!" The dogbot began to scrabble in the sand with his metal paws, sending clouds of silt billowing into the water behind him. *If we can just get Spike free before Crusher makes a move*, Max thought, *we'll have a chance to escape.*

Max looked round, and his heart sank as he saw that the centipede was tightening the circle around them, slowly but surely. Max saw its spiky legs moving beneath the segments, scrabbling in the sand as it drew nearer. Could they free Spike in time?

"Dig faster, Riv!"

"Yes, Max."

"The centipede – do you think it was disturbed by the crystal column falling?" Lia asked. "Why's it out to get us?"

"I bet the Professor put it here to guard the mining operations," Max replied. "We triggered it by attacking the robots."

The giant centipede was frighteningly close. Max's heart sank as he saw that it had formed a complete loop around them with the back half of its body. They were completely surrounded.

It was glowing a brighter green now. The head end rose up and its yellow eyes stared at Max. Its buzzing sounded angry.

We have to try to defend ourselves, Max thought. He looked around for the giant hyperblade that had fallen from his hands when the crystal column fell, but it was nowhere to be seen. He still had his own, much smaller hyperblade at his belt – but would it be any use against a Robobeast as big as Crusher?

Then he remembered that he still had the stinger in the aquabuggy. If he could get to that, it might be powerful enough to fend off the giant centipede.

"Keep digging!" he said to Rivet. "I'm going to get something."

He launched himself upwards and started to swim over the centipede's coils towards the aquabuggy.

"Look out, Max!" Lia shouted.

Max turned to see the centipede's head lunge at him, its metal jaws snapping. They

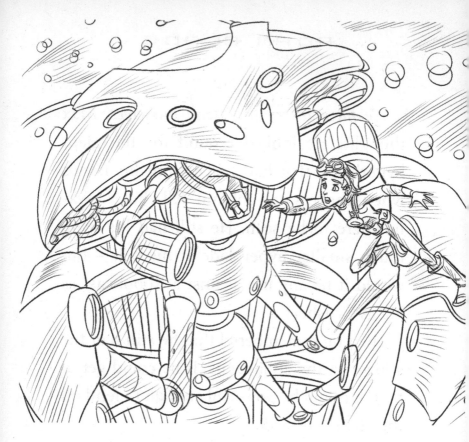

just missed Max's arm.

He pulled the hyperblade from his belt and struck out. Crusher snapped its jaws shut again, pulling the hyperblade from Max's grasp and tossing it aside.

Its jagged mouth re-opened, in what looked like an evil grin. It lunged at him and he tumble-turned out of danger, but the creature rose in the water along with him, its spiky legs bristling from its segmented body.

He tried to dodge past it, but it was too fast and blocked his way. Its legs pointed at Max like giant needles, driving him down to the seabed and inside the loop of its back segments.

The buzzing noise got louder. The loop was tightening. *That's how it deals with its victims*, Max thought. *It surrounds and then crushes them.* It would live up to its name if they couldn't break free.

The upper part of Crusher's body hung above them, needle-like legs hemming them in. It glowed a poisonous green. The yellow eyes in its round head glared down, and its mouth opened hungrily.

We're in big trouble, Max thought. *And now we don't even have a weapon!*

CHAPTER SEVEN

MAX FIGHTS BACK

Rivet was still digging frantically, trying to release Spike from his trap.

"Come on, Rivet!" Lia said. She was crouched by Spike's side, stroking him.

Max saw a flash of movement, on the other side of Crusher. It was Roger, jetting towards them.

"Roger! Help!"

"Good job you got me, ain't it?" Roger said. "Don't worry, I'll soon send that thing to Davy Jones's locker!"

He took his blaster pistol from the belt of his deepsuit, took aim at Crusher's head and fired.

A weak pulse of light came from the muzzle of the blaster. It faded away before it had even reached Crusher.

"Sorry," Roger said. "Must be out of charge."

With a sudden flurry of movement, Spike swam clear of the crystal rock that had been pinning him. Rivet had finally managed to dig deep enough.

"Spike!" said Lia. "Are you all right? Keep still." She examined Spike's bleeding fin carefully. "Can you move that?"

The swordfish's fin slowly wagged up and down.

"Oh, Spike – thank Thallos you're all right!"

"Look out!" Max shouted. The centipede's coil was tightening around them, and there was no way out – Max could almost touch both sides if he stretched out his arms. The sharp metal legs of the upper segments hung above them like a roof of swords. There was no escape that way. They were about to be completely trapped in a robot prison. "We have to hold it back!" he said.

He pushed with all his strength at the centipede's smooth metal body. Lia did the same on the other side. Rivet joined in, struggling to push Crusher back, his propellers whirring. Spike stabbed at the Robobeast with his razor-sharp bill.

But it was no use. Crusher was too strong. The loop tightened pitilessly.

Max had an idea. "Roger!" he shouted. "Get the jellyfish stinger from the aquabuggy!"

"Of course! Bet you're glad now that I didn't let you give it away to the Grundle, aren't you?" Roger said. He jetted away and returned a few moments later with Stinger's robotic tentacle. He was just able to push the tentacle between the centipede's descending swordlike legs and its back segments. Max grabbed it, carefully avoiding the electric sting at the end.

"Quick, Max!" Lia said.

Max thrust the glowing tip of the tentacle
at the giant centipede.

There was a spark and a crackle. Crusher's
buzzing noise went high-pitched, as if it was
squealing in pain. Its legs scrabbled and the
segment Max had touched jerked away.

"Look out, Max!" Rivet barked.

Crusher's upper half lashed down, green-
glowing sword-legs rushing towards Max.

He jabbed upwards with the stinger, hitting one of Crusher's legs. Again there was a flash and a high-pitched buzz. Crusher recoiled, its legs twitching wildly.

Max breathed out a sigh of relief. "All right, we can keep it at bay," he said. "That's bought us some time."

"But we don't have any time to spare!" Lia said. She pointed. "Look!"

Max saw that the mining robots were back at work again. They were attacking another of the crystal columns. Already, he could see a network of cracks. *If this one goes too*, Max thought, *that may be enough to bring the whole cave system down. Then both Hydrophantia and Sumara will be destroyed.*

"You're right," he said. "We can't let any more columns collapse." He turned to Roger. "You have to try to stop those mining robots!"

"Stop them?" Roger said. "Why would I do

that? They're digging out pure, high-grade crystal, worth a fortune on the open market – in my line of work you don't turn your back on treasure!"

"What line of work?" Lia said. "Piracy?"

"I'm not a pirate," Roger said. "I'm, er, a salvage expert."

"Listen!" Max said. "You saw what happened when the last column fell. If this one goes we might not be so lucky. Treasure won't help you if the whole roof comes crashing down on your head."

"Hmm," Roger said. "Maybe you got a point there, boy. All right, I'll see what I can do."

He jetted off towards the crystal column.

"Watch out, Max!" Lia said.

Crusher was tightening the loop again, fast. Max saw the legs scuttling over the sand in a pool of green light, and the smooth metal walls of its body looming.

Max hit it with the stinger. Its legs scrabbled and it moved away a short distance, giving them some breathing space.

Roger had reached the column and was doing his best to pull the robots off, one by one. But every time Roger knocked one off the surface of the crystal column, another moved in to replace it. It didn't help that

Roger kept breaking off from his task to stuff more crystal into his pockets.

"He'll never do it alone," Max said. "We have to get past the centipede so we can stop those robots."

Lia shook her head. "Getting past it won't be enough. It's not going to stand by and watch while we deal with the robots. We're going to have to destroy it."

"You're right," Max said. "But how?"

"What about those aquamines you brought from the Graveyard in Sumara?"

"Of course! Good thinking," said Max. The Graveyard was where the Merryn kept all the human technology they found from shipwrecks. They didn't understand it themselves, and had no use for it. Max had brought some aquamines – high explosives that worked underwater – from the Graveyard. He'd used them to break through into the Cavern of Ghosts. But perhaps they could be used against a Robobeast too...

"I do have some left," he said. "They're stowed in the aquabuggy. But I can't detonate them here, in this confined space. We'd be blown up too!"

"You understand machines," Lia said. "Can't you open Crusher up somehow, get into the control panel – make it let us go?"

Max thought hard, rubbing his chin. "Maybe," he said. "Then if I could lead it away from the columns I could blow it up safely."

Rivet suddenly barked. "Danger!"

Crusher's head segment snaked down through the water, straight at Lia, jaws snapping.

Spike shot in front of her and crashed into Crusher's face. The impact sent the swordfish tumbling back to the ocean floor, but it was

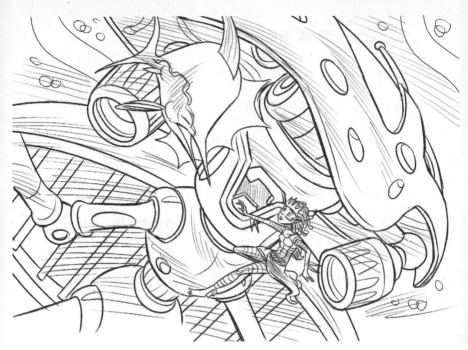

just enough to turn the Robobeast's attack
aside. Its jagged mouth missed Lia's head by
a hair's breadth.

Max thrust the jellyfish stinger upwards.
There was another spark and a crackle. The
upper half of the centipede jerked away again.
Max saw its yellow eyes flare brightly, as if it
was angry. How much longer could he hold
it off? The electrical charge of the stinger
wouldn't last forever. He had to destroy or
disable Crusher, and soon. But how could he

get to its control panel?

"The trouble is," he said to Lia, "it's not going to keep still and let me open it up. It's going to thrash around and throw me off."

"If only you could tie yourself on, somehow..." Lia said.

Max looked at the jellyfish tentacle in his hand. "Maybe we've got a plan," he said.

CHAPTER EIGHT

DRIVING CRUSHER

M ax's brain moved into high gear. For the plan to succeed, they'd all have to work together.

"Roger!" he called.

Roger looked round, pausing from his battle with the mining robots on the column. "What? I'm a little busy here!"

"Swim back to the buggy – get the aquamines! Don't forget the detonator."

"Make your mind up! Do you want me to

fight robots or get aquamines?"

"Aquamines!" Max shouted. He turned to Rivet. "I'm going to get you out of here. As soon as you're free, swim to Roger and get the mines. Take them a long way away from the crystal columns, and bury them in the sand – got it?"

"Yes, Max!" Rivet barked.

"Lia," Max said. "You and Spike attack Crusher. Try to distract it while I find a place to tie myself onto it."

"Right!" said Lia. She and Spike went for the centipede's nearest segment. Lia kicked and beat her fists against the smooth surface, while Spike jabbed with his sharp bill.

Crusher reacted fast. The segment flipped sideways so that its sword-like legs were pointing inwards. They jabbed viciously at Lia and her swordfish. Spike managed to parry the lunge with his bill. Lia only just

darted back in time to avoid being slashed.

Max hit the metal legs with the jellyfish stinger and they retracted.

Lia and Spike quickly moved on to the next segment and attacked again. Crusher was wriggling now, its segments shifting, and for a moment Max saw the join between two segments – a network of jointed, flexible metal tendons.

A moment was all he needed.

He jabbed the stinger at the precise place where the segments joined.

There was a huge flash. Crusher bucked. The two segments parted.

"Quick!" Max said. "Go!"

Lia, Spike and Rivet darted through the gap.

The top half of Crusher was looking down at its bottom half. Its blank robotic face looked almost puzzled, as if it were wondering why its back segments were no longer attached.

Now was his chance.

Max swam up to the head segment and gripped it from behind with his hands and knees. The head waved violently, but before it could throw him off, Max passed the jellyfish tentacle around himself – taking care to keep the stinging end away from him – and wedged each end in the gap between the head and the next segment. The slight stickiness of the robo-tentacle helped keep it in place. It was firm around his waist. Crusher bucked, but couldn't dislodge him.

Max ran his hands over the surface, looking for a panel he could open. There was nothing – just smooth metal. There had to be a way into its workings somehow!

The eyes, he suddenly thought.

He stretched forward as far as the robo-tentacle would allow, feeling his way over the creature's head and down onto its face. He felt the slight heat of an electric eye under his hand.

Crusher reared and twisted, trying to throw him off.

The jellyfish tentacle held fast.

Max felt his way around the eye. He would smash it with his fist if necessary, but it would be easier if it could be removed...

Yes! There was a kind of ridge around the edge, which he was able to turn. He unscrewed it. The eye fell out of the socket, and Max saw it tumble slowly down towards the seabed.

Crusher went wild, bucking and weaving from side to side. *It must be programmed to protect its inner workings at all costs*, Max thought. But there was no way it could shake him off.

He inched forward so that he could see what he was doing. The tentacle stretched, but still held him tightly by his waist.

The eye socket was a dark hole. Max could see a tangle of wires and circuits inside. He put his hand in and felt around. His fingers

encountered a moving lever, mounted in a flexible socket.

The lever shifted from side to side as the centipede swayed from left to right. Then it moved upwards, at the same time as Crusher's head reared up.

Right, Max thought. *I get it. The lever*

controls Crusher's movements.

He gripped the lever and, using all his strength, held it still.

The giant centipede froze.

Slowly, Max pushed the lever downwards.

Crusher's head slowly descended towards the ocean floor. It made a grinding, screeching noise, as if protesting, but its body followed.

Max heard Rivet's electronic bark travelling through the water from a long way off.

"Here, Max! Here!"

He saw the tiny figure of his dogbot way off in the distance. Rivet was far enough from the columns that the explosion wouldn't damage them.

Max turned the lever, directing Crusher towards where Rivet was standing. He was beginning to enjoy himself. There was a strange sense of power at controlling such an enormous Robobeast. *This must be how the Professor feels*, he thought.

Crusher snaked over the seabed, towards where the aquamines were buried.

Lia, sitting on Spike's back, came and glided along beside him. "That's fantastic, Max!"

"Thanks – but there's still a difficult bit," Max said. "We have to get the timing exactly right. Can you get Roger and the detonator?"

"Of course." Lia and Spike darted away. In the distance, Max saw Roger jetting to meet them, and handing over the detonator.

"Here, Max! Here!" Rivet barked. He was standing at the place where he'd buried the aquamines, snuffling at the sand.

Max carefully guided Crusher until it was right over the spot. He held the lever still and the centipede halted.

Lia reappeared beside him. She held up the detonator, a small black control unit with a red touchpad. "Is this it?"

"That's it," said Max. "Get away from here

before you press it. You too, Riv. There's going to be the mother of all explosions!" He'd used three aquamines to break into the Cavern of Ghosts, and that had destroyed a wall of solid rock. There had been six aquamines left, so this explosion was going to be twice as big.

"What about you?" Lia said.

"I have to stay here to keep Crusher in position until the last moment," Max said. "Don't worry. Signal to me as soon as you've pressed the detonator, and that should give me time to get clear."

"If you're sure," said Lia, a little doubtfully.

She and Spike swam off, with Rivet paddling behind them. They stopped in the middle distance. Lia held up the detonator so Max could see.

Max felt the lever trying to jiggle beneath his fingers – almost as if Crusher knew what was about to happen and was struggling to escape. He held on tight, not letting the lever move.

"Ready, Max?" called Lia.

"Ready," said Max. He knew that when the plunger went down he'd have about ten seconds to swim clear. That should be enough, provided he kept very close to the ground – the full force of the explosion would rise upwards and pass over his head.

He saw Lia raise her hand and press the touchpad.

He let go of Crusher's lever, and tried to lift the jellyfish tentacle and kick off.

Crusher began to buck and squirm, but the tentacle wouldn't budge.

I can't move!

The soft, sticky tentacle held him tight.

He had only ten seconds to get free.

Less – nine, eight...

He pulled frantically at the tentacle. It stretched, but it wouldn't break. Crusher was buzzing again, sounding more angry than ever.

Max felt the blood pounding in his ears.

Seven.

Six...

CHAPTER NINE

SWALLOWED ALIVE

Crusher reared up again, trying in vain to shake Max off. It had no idea of the explosion that was coming and it wasn't moving out of the blast zone. *And neither am I*, thought Max desperately.

He strained against the jellyfish tentacle, wriggling, tugging at it, trying to peel it away from the centipede segment. It wouldn't budge.

Five, four...

"Looks like you could use a little help!" a voice said.

Max looked over his shoulder to see Roger, holding the large hyperblade from Shredder's leg in his hands. Relief surged through Max.

Roger brought the hyperblade down hard and fast, and the tentacle split in two. The pirate grabbed Max's arm and pulled him

away. The rockets on his boots fired up. He and Max zoomed away from the centipede, keeping close to the seabed.

A couple of seconds later Max heard the *BOOM* of the explosion. It felt as though his eardrums had been punched.

Then he felt as though a giant hand was pushing and lifting him with incredible force. He was carried away from Roger and whirled headlong in an undersea tidal wave. He saw bits of Crusher flying past him in the water – detached legs, fragments of the outer casing and bits of its inner workings.

Crusher's one-eyed head was hurtling straight for Max. It was heavy enough to do him a lot of damage, even though the Robobeast had been destroyed. He twisted to the side just in time, and felt the swoosh of the water as the head shot past.

When the force of the wave finally died down, Max steadied himself and looked around. Roger was nowhere to be seen. Max hoped his jet-powered boots had carried him safely away from the blast.

Pieces of Crusher lay on the seabed. Max saw his own hyperblade lying there among the debris, and felt a surge of joy, as if he'd met an old friend. It looked undamaged; the solid vernium blade wasn't even scratched. He picked it up and tucked it in his belt.

Next to where the hyperblade had lain was a piece of Crusher's shell, with one of the sword-like legs still attached. *That might be worth having*, Max thought, remembering how useful Shredder's leg had turned out to be. He picked it up, then began to swim back towards the Crystal Forest.

He saw Lia, Spike and Rivet ahead of him, and called to them.

"Max!" Lia said. "You made it!"

Rivet paddled up and licked Max's arm with his rasping metal tongue.

"I wouldn't have made it without Roger," Max said. "He saved me. Has anyone seen him?"

"I'm here, shipmates!" Roger said, arriving beside them.

"Thanks," Max said. "You saved my life!"

"Just repaying a favour," Roger said. "You helped me out with those Deadly Rainbow fish, remember? Old Roger never forgets a favour. Anyway, it looks like we've destroyed Crusher too. Mission accomplished, me hearties!"

"Not quite," Max said. "First we have to stop those mining robots."

The little black boxy robots were still hacking away at the crystal column, undeterred by the explosion.

"Let's go!" Lia said.

They swooped down on the robots. Spike stabbed and chopped at them with his bill. Rivet chomped them with his iron jaws. Max sliced the robots' arms off with his hyperblade, while Roger used the large blade salvaged from Shredder. Lia grabbed a fallen pickaxe and smashed at their heads.

It didn't take them long to disable all the

mining robots. Deactivated, they sank to the foot of the crystal columns, where they lay on the ocean floor like dead beetles.

The crystal column was cracked and scarred, but still standing.

Max let out a huge breath. Only now did he realise how much effort he'd put in. He was exhausted and his arms and legs were aching. But he felt good. They'd defeated Crusher and put a stop to the Professor's mining operation.

"Now it's mission accomplished!" he said. They had stopped the cavern roof from caving in. Hydrophantia and Sumara were safe.

For now.

"We need to press on," Lia said. "We're heading for the Professor's lair, remember?"

Max felt a pang in his heart. They'd found no trace of his mother. But Lia was right. They needed to stop the Professor, before he caused any more trouble. "Agreed – we have to go east," he said. "That way." He pointed to where the cliff fell away, behind the Crystal Forest.

"Reckon I'll come with you," Roger said. "There may be rich pickings!"

"Let's go, then!" Max said. "Come on, Riv!"
He swam down to retrieve his aquabuggy.
He strapped the piece of Crusher with its
sword-like leg to the back. After a moment's
thought, he took his mother's conch off the
back, and tucked it away inside his tunic, for
safekeeping. Rivet climbed on. Max stepped
on the accelerator and the aquabuggy moved
off, just above the ocean floor.

Lia and Spike swam down to join them.
Roger kept pace on the other side of the
aquabuggy, powered by his jetboots.

They travelled out of the forest, over
the edge of the cliff they'd seen when they
first arrived. Below them the ocean was so
deep that the bottom couldn't be seen. Max
looked back and saw the smooth grey edge
of the cliff they'd just passed over. Slowly
they dipped downwards, until the top was
no longer visible.

"Roger," Max said. "You said this was where you met my mother." He was determined to find out as much as he could. "How long ago was it?"

"Arr, well, let me see, Max lad..." Roger began. "It must have been—"

"Can anyone – feel anything?" Lia interrupted.

Roger frowned. "Feel anything?"

Suddenly Max realised that they were speeding up. Something was pulling them downwards, and now back, towards the base of the grey cliff.

"What's happening?" he asked. "Lia, what is this?"

"I don't know," she said. "An ocean current, maybe?" But she didn't sound convinced.

"Avast!" Roger said. "I don't like this!" He pointed. "Look where it's taking us!"

Looking back, Max saw the grey cliff loom

back into view. They were being dragged back towards it, into some kind of vast cavern. A curved range of white peaks ringed the entrance, as big as mountains. They were strangely regular – very sharp and pointed and all much the same size.

"Everybody swim!" Roger shouted. "Swim for your lives!"

Max heard the urgency in his voice. He tried to drive the aquabuggy against the current, but it was too strong. Rivet's propellers stepped up a gear, but he too was carried along at the same rate. Max saw Lia and Spike straining to get away, but even they couldn't make any headway. Roger fired up his rocket-powered boots. The jets streamed out behind him, but it made absolutely no difference. The current had them in its grip, and was dragging them through the water at the same steady pace. They could fight all they liked, but they couldn't do anything about it.

"We're in trouble, shipmates!" Roger said. Under his deepsuit helmet his face was pale. "I don't reckon we're getting out of this – and me with my pockets full of treasure, too! I don't reckon I'll be getting a chance to spend any of it now."

"What's going on?" Max yelled. "What are those hills?"

"They're not hills, boy!" Roger snapped. "Haven't you got eyes in your head?"

Max looked closer. Behind the white mounds was an area of red, and behind that what looked like a massive black tunnel. Above, there was another row of white mountains – upside down this time – and the smooth grey cliff rising up...

Suddenly, something clicked in Max's brain, and the whole scene made sense.

Horrible sense.

The hills weren't hills – they were teeth!

The red area was a giant tongue, the tunnel an enormous throat. And the grey cliff above them must be the snout of some immense beast, bigger than a whale, bigger than anything Max would have believed possible.

Max remembered the gigantic creature that had been sleeping beneath the Sea Ghost city of Spectron. He had heard its slow heartbeat, and felt its cool, smooth hide under the sand. The explosion must have woken it!

He heard a low, grumbling sound, like distant thunder.

"What's happening, Max?" Rivet asked.

"Something bad," Max said.

The monstrous creature's mouth was sucking them in. The teeth and throat were getting closer, looming larger with every second that passed.

He redoubled his efforts to swim against
the current, and saw the others do the same.
It was hopeless.

They had defeated Crusher and saved the

Crystal Forest – but now they were going to be swallowed alive by that massive mouth. And there wasn't a thing that any of them could do about it.

In the next Sea Quest
adventure, Max must face

MANGLER
THE DARK MENACE

Read on for an exclusive extract...

Sharp white peaks rose through the gloomy water as far as Max could see. They weren't mountains – they were enormous teeth. Max was staring into the mouth of the most gigantic sea creature he'd ever seen. Bigger than any ship built in his home city of Aquora, maybe even bigger than the city itself. A pink tongue thrust towards them, then slipped back into the black hole of the monster's throat.

"We're going to be swallowed!" Lia cried.

A rush of water gripped Max like a powerful undertow, sucking him through the water. He lost his grip on the aquabuggy and it spun away until it looked smaller than a child's toy.

"Swim for your lives!" said Roger. "Every sailor for himself!" He turned and swam against the current, boot-thrusters churning bubbles as he shot away.

Typical! thought Max.

"After him!" Lia shouted.

She clung close to Spike's back as the swordfish strained to fight the powerful surge of water. Rivet's leg propellers roared. Max kicked as hard as he could, but already he could feel that the current was too strong. Roger was a speck in the distance, but he seemed to be getting bigger again. *Even his thrusters aren't strong enough.*

"Hold, Max!" barked Rivet, as the current dragged him down beside Max.

Max gripped his dogbot's collar, but he could feel the rush of water growing in strength like a gale. They were being sucked further into the creature's mouth, faster and faster.

It can't end like this! thought Max. *Not after everything we've done...*

SEA QUEST ®

Look out for all the books in
Sea Quest Series 3:

THE PRIDE OF BLACKHEART

TETRAX THE SWAMP CROCODILE
NEPHRO THE ICE LOBSTER
FINARIA THE SAVAGE SEA SNAKE
CHAKROL THE OCEAN HAMMER

OUT IN MARCH 2014!

Don't miss the
BRAND NEW
Special Bumper Edition:

STENGOR
THE CRAB MONSTER

978 1 40831 852 2

OUT IN NOVEMBER 2013

WIN AN EXCLUSIVE
GOODY BAG

In every Sea Quest book the Sea Quest logo is
hidden in one of the pictures. Find the logos in books
5–8, make a note of which pages they appear on and
go online to enter the competition at

www.seaquestbooks.co.uk

Each month we will put all of the correct entries into a draw
and select one winner to receive a special Sea Quest goody bag.

You can also send your entry on a postcard to:

**Sea Quest Competition, Orchard Books,
338 Euston Road, London, NW1 3BH**

Don't forget to include your name and address!

GOOD LUCK

Closing Date: December 30th 2013

DARE YOU DIVE IN?

www.seaquestbooks.co.uk

Deep in the water lurks a new breed of Beast.

Dive into the new Sea Quest website to play games, download activities and wallpapers and read all about Robobeasts, Max, Lia, the Professor and much, much more.

Sign up to the newsletter at www.seaquestbooks.co.uk to receive exclusive extra content, members-only competitions and the most up-to-date information about Sea Quest.

IF YOU LIKE SEA QUEST, YOU'LL LOVE BEAST QUEST!

Series 1: COLLECT THEM ALL!

An evil wizard has enchanted the magical beasts of Avantia. Only a true hero can free the beasts and save the land. Is Tom the hero Avantia has been waiting for?

978 1 84616 483 5

978 1 84616 482 8

978 1 84616 484 2

978 1 84616 486 6

978 1 84616 485 9

978 1 84616 487 3

DON'T MISS THE
BRAND NEW SERIES OF:

FREE COLLECTOR CARDS INSIDE!

Series 14: THE CURSED DRAGON

978 1 40832 920 7

978 1 40832 921 4

978 1 40832 922 1

978 1 40832 923 8

OUT IN JANUARY 2014!